The Berenstain Bears® and the SPOOKY OLD HOUSE

Stan & Jan Berenstain

Reader's Digest **Kids**

Westport, Connecticut

One day, when the Bears were in
their yard, a letter came.
"Who is it from?" asked Mama Bear.

"It's from Mr. Bruno Brown," said Papa Bear. "He's a big lawyer in town."

"Why is he writing to us?" asked Mama.

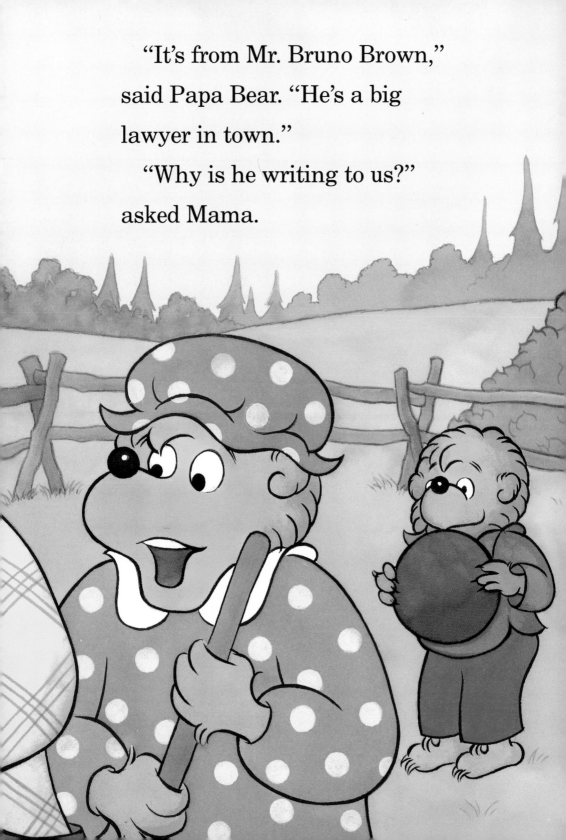

As Papa read the letter, his eyes
grew wider and wider.

"What does the letter say?" Mama
asked.

"It says that rich Widow McBear passed away and left us a gift," said Papa.

"My goodness," said Mama. "What sort of gift?"

"That's the trouble," said
Papa. "She left us a house—
the spooky old house on
Spook Hill."

"G-g-golly!" said Brother.

"D-d-double golly!" said Sister.

"My goodness!" said Mama.

"But that's not all," said Papa. "To get our gift, we must go to the spooky old house in the dark of night."

The Bear family thought about the spooky old house on top of Spook Hill. It was such a spooky thought, it made them shiver.

"Hmm," said Papa. "There's a P.S.!"

"What does it say?" asked Mama.

"It says that to get our gift we must go to the spooky old house on the *next* dark night!"

Sister looked up at the sky. "The sky is cloudy. So the clouds will hide the moon and stars."

"Which means," said Papa with another shiver, "that the next dark night *will be tonight*!"

The Bears thought about the spooky old house again.

Brother thought there might be ghosts in the spooky old house.

Sister thought there might be goblins in the spooky old house.

Papa thought there might be
monsters in the spooky old house.

But Mama thought it was
just an empty, falling-apart
old house. She thought it
could be put to good use.

That night the Bears stood at the bottom of Spook Hill, looking up at the spooky old house.

"I'm afraid," said Brother. "I'm afraid there are ghosts in the spooky old house."

"I'm afraid, too," said Sister. "I'm afraid there are goblins in the spooky old house."

"I'm not afraid," said Papa. "But I'm a *little* worried that there may be monsters in the spooky old house."

"Stuff and nonsense!" said Mama. "That's just an empty, falling-apart old house. It's ours now. We should put it to good use! So, follow me!" And up Spook Hill they went.

Brother was wrong. There were no ghosts in the spooky old house.

Sister was wrong. There were no goblins in the spooky old house.

Papa was wrong. There were no monsters in the spooky old house.

And Mama was wrong, too! The spooky old house WAS NOT EMPTY!

Looking out the windows of the
spooky old house on top of Spook Hill
were lots of eyes. Lots and lots of little
eyes—and one pair of big eyes!

The little eyes belonged to the many, many bats who lived in the spooky old house on top of Spook Hill.

The big eyes belonged to Raggedy Tom, who had made the spooky old house his home.

As the Bears came closer and closer, Raggedy Tom and the bats became more and more afraid.

"*Creak! Creak!*" went the wooden floor as the Bears walked across the porch.

"*Rattle! Rattle!*" went the rusty old knob as Mama tried the door.

"*Squeeek!*" went the old door as Mama pulled it open.

"*WHOOSH!*" went the many, many bats as they flew out the open door.

"Ghosts!" shouted Brother.

"Goblins!" shouted Sister.

"Monsters!" shouted Papa.

"Help!" shouted Raggedy Tom.

"Everybody calm down,"
said Mama as she lit a candle.

And with the help of Raggedy Tom, that's what the Bears did.

The spooky old house got fixed up, cleaned up, and painted until it looked like new.

The spooky old house is now the Bear Country Cub Club. Raggedy Tom takes care of it, and he has a room of his own. The bats work all night and sleep all day, so everybody gets along just fine.